MW01106444

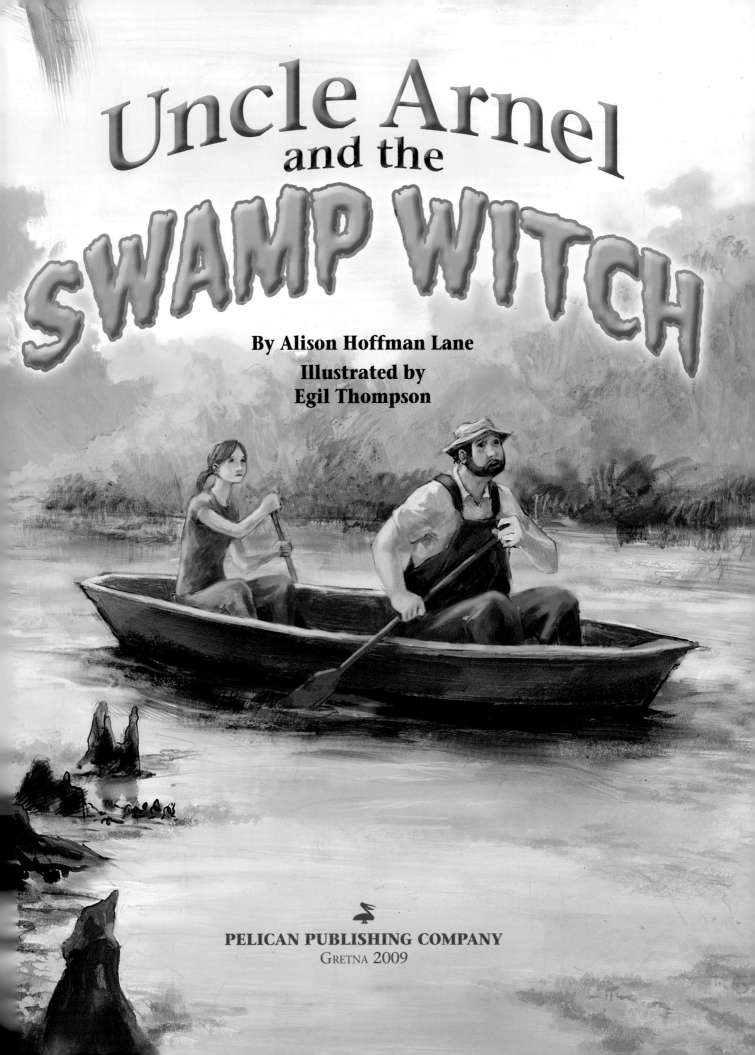

Uncle Arnel
and the
SWAMP WITCH

By Alison Hoffman Lane

Illustrated by
Egil Thompson

PELICAN PUBLISHING COMPANY
GRETNA 2009

To my children, David, Maria, Catherine, and Mary Frances, who inspired me to write in the first place by giving life to my life. And to my husband, Mike, for his support in making this dream of publication a reality for me.

The word "Pelican" and the depiction of a pelican are trademarks of Pelican Publishing Company, Inc., and are registered in the U.S. Patent and Trademark Office.

Library of Congress Cataloging-in-Publication Data

Lane, Alison Hoffman.
  Uncle Arnel and the Swamp Witch / by Alison Hoffman Lane ; illustrated by Egil Thompson.
     p. cm.
  Summary: Marie and Uncle Arnel realize all the stories about the Swamp Witch are true when they come face to face with her in the Cajun bayou.
  ISBN 978-1-58980-644-3 (hardcover : alk. paper) [1. Witches—Fiction 2. Bayous—Fiction. 3. Uncles—Fiction. 4. Louisiana—Fiction.] I. Thompson, Egil, ill. II. Title.
  PZ7.2317578Un 2009
  [E]—dc22

                    2008030450

Printed in Singapore
Published by Pelican Publishing Company, Inc.
1000 Burmaster Street, Gretna, Louisiana 70053

"Uncle Arnel, Uncle Arnel," I yelled. "There she is! The Swamp Witch Aunt Cherie warned us about!" Uncle Arnel grabbed me, and we dove under the big fallen cypress log, holding our breath.

For many generations, here, in the Acadian swamps of Louisiana, a story has been told of a Swamp Witch and the awful power she possesses. We had many a fais-dodo where the story was passed on.

Some Cajuns believe the stories are told just to frighten the young ones; others believe it is their duty to pass down the story as part of tradition.

My name is Marie. I live with my Aunt Cherie and Uncle Arnel. I believe in tradition.

Whatever the case, we never knew she actually existed until this day. If the tales of her terrible power were also true, our entire Cajun family, including Uncle Arnel and me, would become twelve inches tall, at best, were she to gaze upon us. I shuddered at the thought.

We remained still, as if frozen, hiding under that big cypress log, afraid to move. All was silent. The gentle swamp breeze swept through the long, hanging Spanish moss. A snowy white egret with long, skinny legs took flight in the distance. One turtle, then another, and another plopped into the water from their perches as the daylight began to fade.

A nutria was heard scampering quickly through the decaying vegetation that is always found along a swamp path. Frozen with fear, we did not dare move even after a nearby gator gave a throaty growl and splashed the murky water with his powerful tail.

After a long while, Uncle Arnel cautiously looked up. At first, all he could see was the moss-draped cypress trees. But, something in the distant trees seemed very odd. There, in the evening cast of enveloping fog, was the Swamp Witch. She moved with an eerie motion, making it hard to determine if she was moving closer or farther away from the cypress tree.

Uncle Arnel could not establish the witch's size. Her skin, if you could call that skin, seemed to have no color. It was hard to know where her hair stopped and her clothing began. Was she floating with the fog, or was she walking? Were the Swamp Witch's arms swaying with the breeze, or was the movement of her arms causing the breeze? With her presence, a strange chill took over the air.

Suddenly, much to Uncle Arnel's surprise, he was caught in her gaze! At what moment their eyes locked, it is hard to know. Did she turn her head, or was she always looking in his direction? Sure as there are red beans and rice on Mondays, there they were, face to face.

Then the Swamp Witch whispered in an almost metallic, coarse, deep voice, sounding neither male nor female, *"Pauvre ti bête,"* meaning "Poor little thing." The witch's voice alone terrified us and sent shivers slowly and deeply right down our spines. But, now, Uncle Arnel was looking into her eyes, those hideous eyes . . . those empty, soulless, pitiful eyes!

After a long piercing stare, the witch said, *"C'est tout,"* or "That is all." A putrid odor, which seemed to come from her horrid stare, filled the air. As quickly as she had appeared, she disappeared, leaving behind the rotting odor and a lingering unnatural chill.

The Swamp Witch's curse sent Uncle Arnel and Marie swirling as if lost in a shoreless sea. Then they lay still, aching all over. Several moments later, the feeling passed, and Uncle Arnel bravely stood up as tall as he could, which, of course, was now all of twelve inches!

I, too, had shrunk to a miniscule size. Although shocked by his new size, being true to the enduring spirit of the Cajun people, Uncle Arnel smiled and said, "Marie, *lâche pas la patate, allons,*" which means "Do not give up, let's go."

The journey back home was quite the adventure because now we were dwarfed by everything around us. The saw palmettos were huge, and the cypress trees were now more the size of the giant redwoods I once read about.

We came across a crawfish hole, which was enormous. Now cautious of our surroundings, we ran when a crawfish peeked out from his hole. To us he was like a giant lobster, and his claws looked frightening.

We had to remind ourselves that everything around us was its normal size, and we were the ones who were "petite" or little. The distance back home had now tripled or even quadrupled.

Our pirogue was tied in the bayou at the edge of a marsh. Earlier today, while we were on our usual outing, enjoying the swamp, we had simply walked across the marsh, as we often did. But, now, as we stood on the marsh's edge, we wondered how we were going to cross the marsh and manage our normal-size pirogue?

Getting home was turning out to be more of a challenge than we first realized.

As we sat on the marsh's edge and contemplated the situation, a turtle appeared out of nowhere. For the second time today, we sat stunned. She had kind, soft, friendly eyes, and we quickly felt as if we were with a friend.

Then, much to our astonishment, the turtle spoke. Yes, I said the turtle spoke! Not only did she speak, we understood her, and, when we spoke, she understood us! The Swamp Witch's curse not only made us petite, but also enabled us to talk and understand the critters living in our swamp and bayou. The turtle introduced herself as Myrtle, and, best of all, she had the solution to our problem.

Myrtle invited us to climb on her back and offered to take us across the marsh to our pirogue in the bayou. She was quite comfortable to sit upon, and her shell had little bumps, which served as saddle horns for Uncle Arnel and me. Her movements were smooth and gentle. We enjoyed our ride.

As we approached the bayou and could see our pirogue, we hollered and yelled, "Yippee!" Our pirogue was there, and it was our size. We supposed that the curse of the Swamp Witch touched not only us, but all of our belongings, too. We thanked our new friend, and, as we climbed into the pirogue, Myrtle promised she would come for dinner sometime at our cabin on the other side of the bayou.

When we arrived home, *Tante* (Aunt) Cherie was standing on the front porch next to her pet raccoon, Ralph.

Only now, she and Ralph Raccoon were the same size, and they were talking. The Swamp Witch's curse had spread quickly!

However, there was something not even the Swamp Witch could touch, for *Tante* Cherie's smile and warm hugs were as big as ever. The smell of the gumbo cooking on the stove held wonderful memories and boosted our spirits. We were all different yet very much the same.

There are many tales in
the Louisiana swamps, but this
tale is not a tale at all, it is the truth.

We are now indeed "poor little things." Under the witch's curse, we begin our adventures in the Acadian swamps of Louisiana as petit people. *"Laissez les bons temps rouler,"* "Let the good times roll!"

Glossary

Allons (al-lohn): Let's go

Bayou (bahy-oo): A slow-moving body of water in low-lying areas.

Ca c'est bon (sa-say-bohn): That is good

Cajun (key-juhn): Canadian French people who settled in the bayous of Southern Louisiana after they left Nova Scotia in the 1700s. They are hospitable people who live simply but have great food, music, dances, and traditions.

Crawfish (kraw-fish): Freshwater crustaceans resembling lobsters

Cypress (sahy-pruhs): Tall, evergreen tree that grows in the shallow waters of swamps in the southeast United States. The tree's roots grow above the water level and are called cypress knees.

Egret (ee-grit): About twenty-four inches tall with long legs and a long neck, this bird can be found in marshes, swamps, shorelines, or ponds.

Merci (mer-see): Thank you

Nutria (noo-tree-uh): A large semiaquatic rodent with a long beaverlike tail that can weigh up to twenty pounds.

Pauvre ti bête (pove-tee-bet): Poor little thing

Petite (puh-teet): Little

Pirogue (pee-rohg): A handmade canoe-style wooden boat.

Red Beans and Rice: Traditionally, in New Orleans and the surrounding south Louisiana region, red beans and rice was cooked on wash day (Mondays) using leftover ham bones from Sunday's dinner. Even today on Mondays, red beans and rice can be found in many area homes and restaurants.

Swamp (swomp): Wet, spongy areas growing only certain plants and trees.

Tante (taunt): Aunt